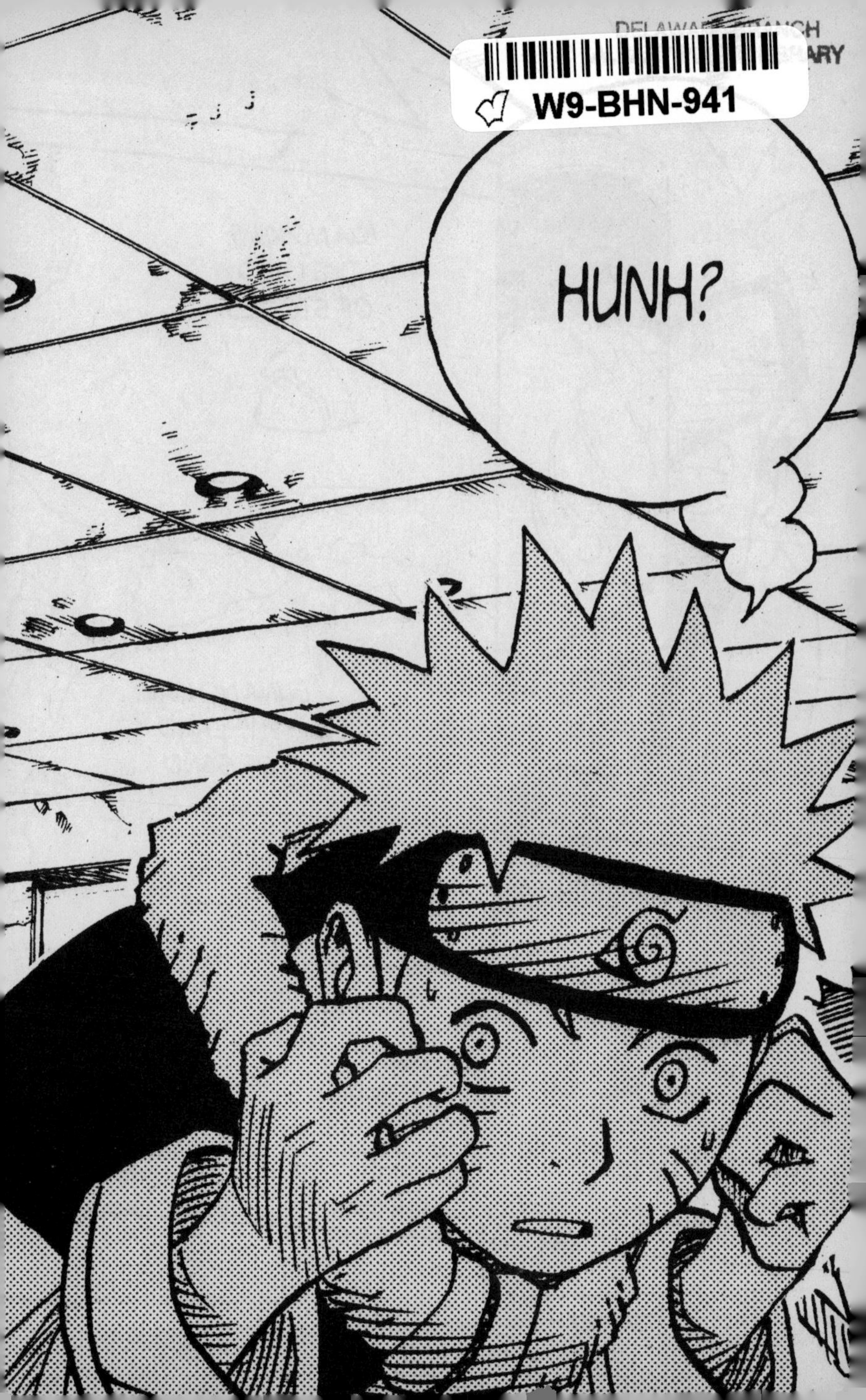
HUNH?

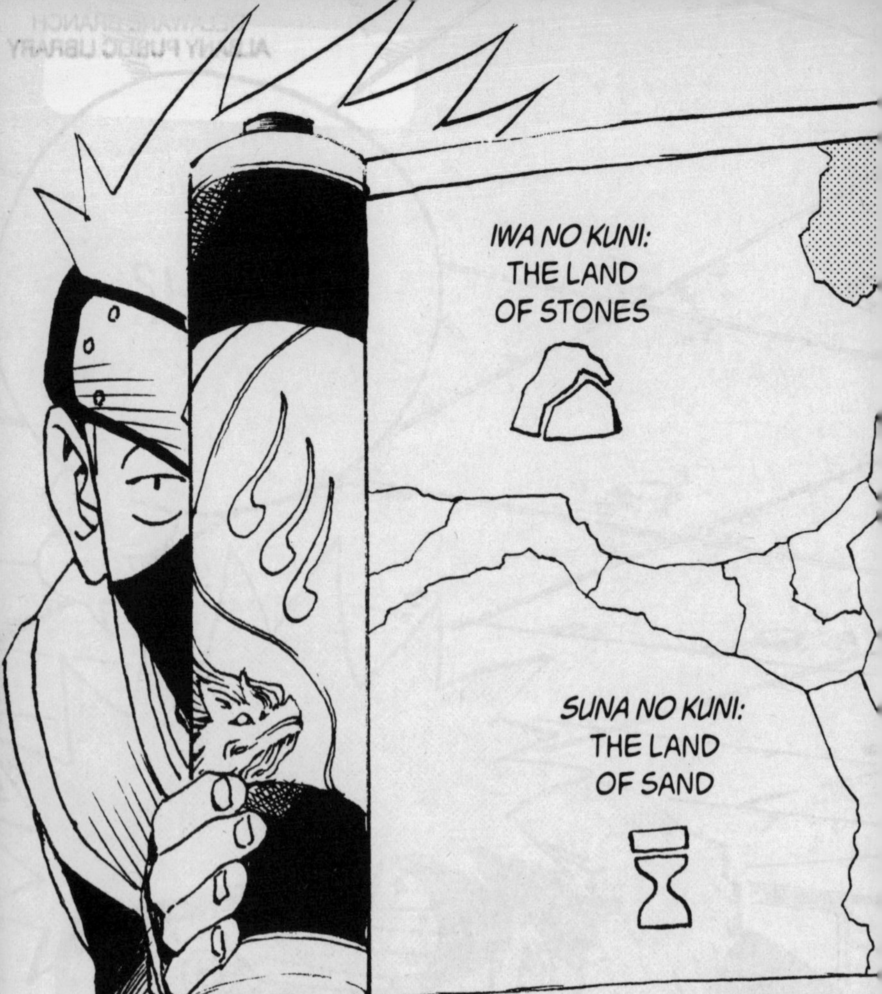
IWA NO KUNI:
THE LAND
OF STONES
SUNA NO KUNI:
THE LAND
OF SAND

THE FIVE LANDS

THE FIRE SHADOW

KONOHA NO KUNI KONOHARGURE NO SATO:

VILLAGE HIDDEN IN THE LEAVES

THE WATER SHADOW

KIRO NO KUNI KIRIGAKURE NO SATO:

VILLAGE HIDDEN IN THE MIST

KUMO NO KUNI:
THE LAND OF
THE CLOUDS

KIRO NO KUNI:
THE LAND OF
MIST AND FOG

KONOHA NO KUNI:
THE LAND OF
TREE AND LEAF

THE LIGHTNING SHADOW

*KUMO NO KUNI
KUMOGAKURE
NO SATO:*

**VILLAGE HIDDEN
IN THE CLOUDS**

THE WIND SHADOW

*SUNA NO KUNI
SUNAGAKURE
NO SATO:*

**VILLAGE HIDDEN
IN THE SAND**

THE EARTH SHADOW

*IWA NO KUNI
IWAGAKURE
NO SATO:*

**VILLAGE HIDDEN
IN THE SHADOW**

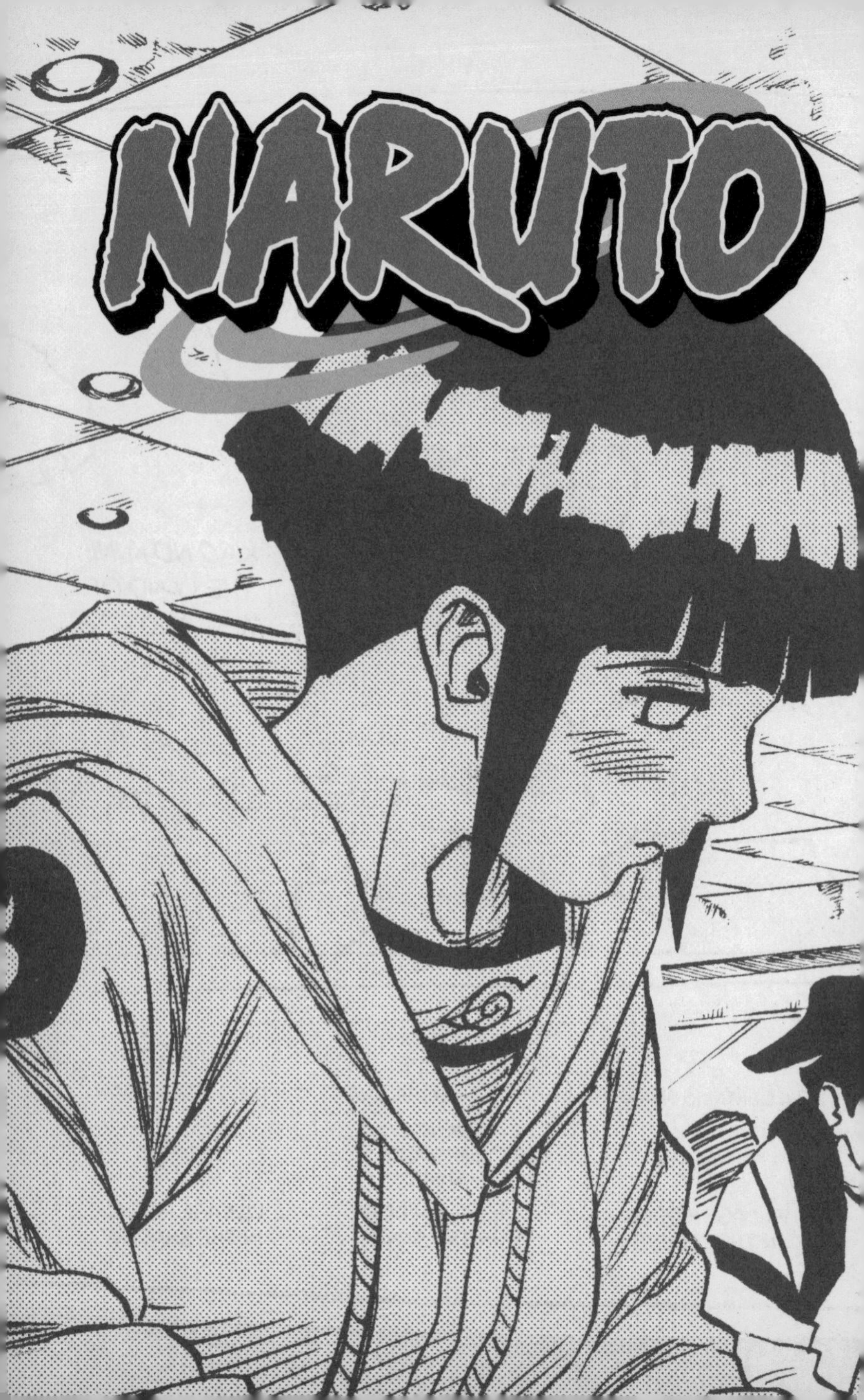
NARUTO

NARUTO THE FIRST TEST
CHAPTER BOOK 10

Illustrations: Masashi Kishimoto
Design: Courtney Utt

Published by VIZ Media, LLC
P.O. Box 77010
San Francisco, CA 94107

www.viz.com

West, Tracey, 1965-
 The first test / original story by Masashi Kishimoto; adapted by
Tracey West; [illustrations, Masashi Kishimoto].
   p. cm. -- (Naruto; [10])
 "A VIZ Kids Book."
 Summary: As the Chunin Exams begin, Naruto is surprised to find that the first is a written test, and if
he cannot control his wisecracking ways he and his friends will remain junior ninjas for another year.
 ISBN 978-1-4215-2320-0
 [1. Examinations--Fiction. 2. Conduct of life--Fiction. 3. Ninja--Fiction.
4. Japan--Fiction.] I. Kishimoto, Masashi, 1974- II. Title.
PZ7.W51937Fjj 2009
[Fic]--dc22
                2009004097

Printed in the U.S.A.
First printing, November 2009

THE *CHÛNIN* JOURNEYMAN NINJA SELECTION EXAM
RULES FOR PART ONE

(1) EACH APPLICANT BEGINS WITH A PERFECT
SCORE OF TEN POINTS. THERE ARE TEN
QUESTIONS WORTH ONE POINT APIECE.
A POINT IS SUBTRACTED FOR EVERY
INCORRECT ANSWER. THE GRADING SYSTEM
IS ENTIRELY BASED ON A PRINCIPLE
OF PENALIZATION.

(2) THE EXAM IS A TEAM EVENT.
WHAT MATTERS IS HOW CLOSE EACH THREE-
NINJA CELL CAN COME TO RETAINING ITS
INITIAL THIRTY POINTS.

(3) ANYONE CAUGHT ATTEMPTING TO CHEAT OR
AIDING AND ABETTING A CHEATER WILL LOSE
TWO POINTS FOR EACH OFFENSE.

(4) ANYONE WHO HAS NO POINTS LEFT AT THE
TEST'S END--WHETHER DUE TO BEING
CAUGHT CHEATING OR TO AN INABILITY TO
ANSWER ANY OF THE QUESTIONS CORRECTLY--
WILL AUTOMATICALLY FAIL; IF A SINGLE
INDIVIDUAL FAILS, THE REMAINING TWO
MEMBERS OF THAT PERSON'S CELL WILL BE
FAILED AS WELL.

THE STORY SO FAR

Young ninja-in-training Naruto, Sasuke, and Sakura are ready to take the Chunin Selection Exam to become the next level of ninja: chunin, also known as journeymen shinobi. They're at Ninja Academy, waiting for things to start. The place is crowded with junior ninja eager to take the exam.

They meet Kabuto, a ninja who has taken the exam six times and failed. Kabuto shows them a deck of cards with info about the ninja who are competing. Kabuto says they're all tough. The only ones he isn't sure about are from the Village Hidden in Sound.

Naruto doesn't care how skilled his competitors are. He's confident that he's going to beat them all, one by one!

BUT, HERE GOES NOTHING...

PO

Naruto
ナルト

Naruto is training to be a ninja. He's a bit of a clown. But deep down, he's serious about becoming the world's greatest shinobi!

Sakura
春野サクラ

Naruto and Sasuke's classmate. She has a crush on Sasuke, who ignores her. In return, she picks on Naruto, who has a crush on *her*.

HARUNO SAKURA. A TOTAL BABE, BUT THAT'S THE PROBLEM...

Sasuke
うちはサスケ

The top student in Naruto's class and a member of the prestigious Uchiha clan.

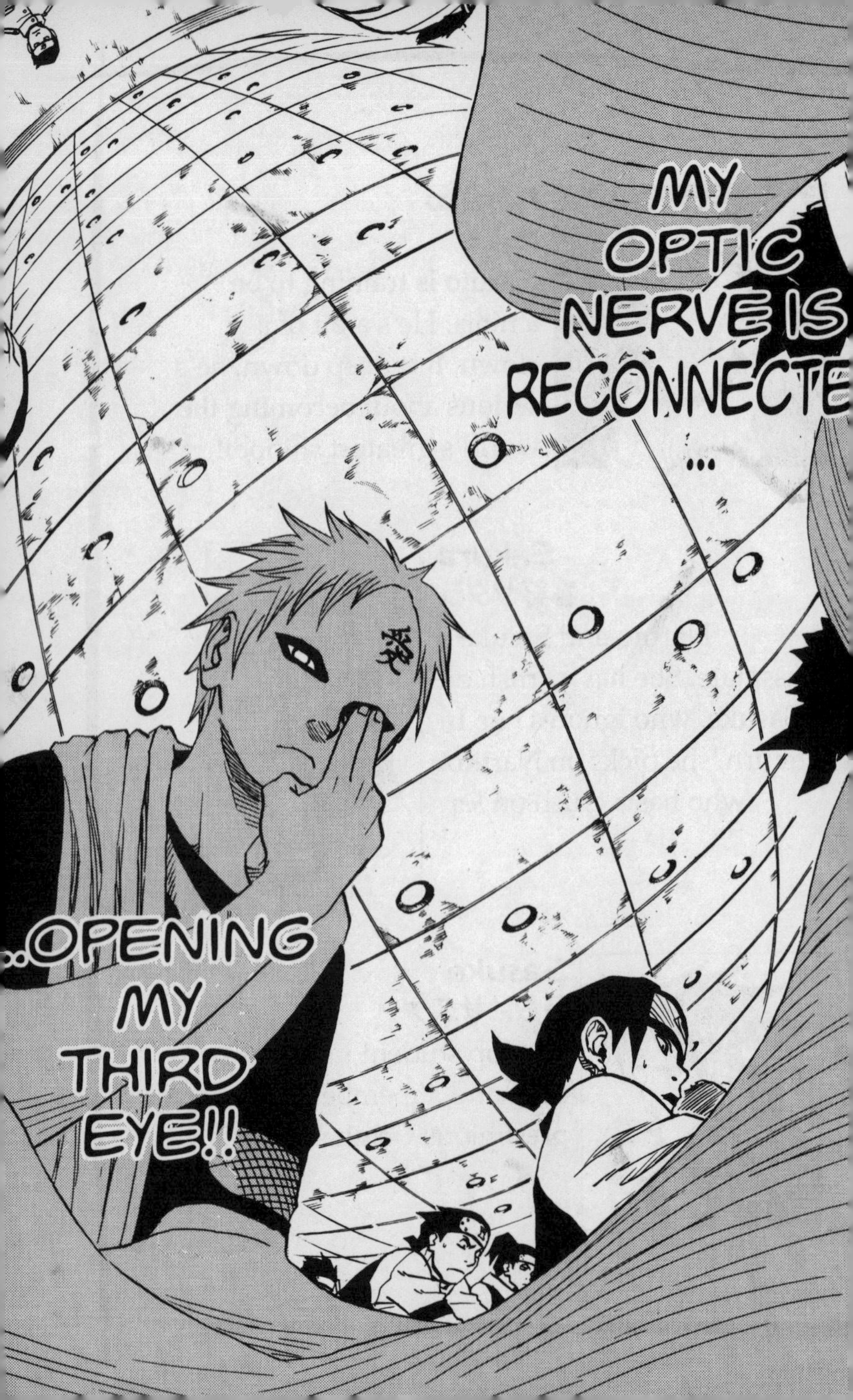
MY OPTIC NERVE IS RECONNECTE
...
..OPENING MY THIRD EYE!!

"MY NAME is Naruto Uzumaki, and none of you are gonna beat me!"

Naruto made the announcement in his loudest voice. Every eye in room 301 turned and glared at him.

Naruto, Sasuke, and Sakura had come to Ninja Academy to take the exam to become journeymen ninja—*chunin*. The three of them were all from the Leaf Village and also members of Squad Seven. They would take the test as a team. The room was filled with other junior ninja, or *genin*, from every village. They looked different and had different skills. But they all had one thing in common—they all thought they were going to win.

A room full of ninja was a dangerous place to be. There were plenty of ninja itching to fight to prove how tough they were. Most of the genin were trying to lay low. They didn't want any trouble before the exams started.

With his bright orange jumpsuit and spiky yellow hair, Naruto already had a hard time blending in. Now he had the attention of everyone in the room.

Ino, another ninja from Leaf Village, looked annoyed.

"What's his problem?" she asked. She angrily jabbed Sakura with her elbow.

Sakura's cheeks turned as pink as her hair. *Typical*, she thought. *He's too stupid to know this is going to cause problems.*

Naruto was grinning. "That felt great!"

Sasuke, Naruto's other squad member, frowned. "Oh please!" Sasuke's dark hair and eyes matched his personality. He was serious about everything, especially being a ninja. If Naruto messed up, then Squad Seven would fail.

A quiet fell over the room as the rest of the genin studied Naruto.

"Didn't we meet him earlier?" asked Kankuro, a tall ninja with purple markings painted on his face. He spoke to Gaara, his fellow squad member from the Village Hidden in the Sand.

The day before, Kankuro had some fun bullying some little kids who hung around with Naruto. Naruto had tried to stop him—but it was Sasuke who succeeded.

Across the room, a ninja named Neji nudged his squad member, Rock Lee.

"Maybe you were too easy on him, Lee," Neji said, smiling. "Kid's got some life in him."

Rock Lee scowled. He and his squad were from the same village as Naruto—Leaf Village. Rock Lee had battled Sasuke on the way to room 301. He thought Sasuke was the top ninja in Squad Seven. Who did this Naruto kid think he was?

One ninja squad looked past Naruto. They glared at Kabuto, a ninja with glasses who wore his long hair in a ponytail. The ninja was older than most of the kids in the room. He had taken the test six times in a row—and failed. Kabuto had info cards on every ninja taking the test that year—except for three.

The three ninja from the Village Hidden in Sound were dressed in camouflage. They stayed at the back of the crowd, away from everyone else. They had heard Kabuto say bad things about their village.

"So everyone thinks our unknown little village is from some backwater country," said the first genin, a tall ninja with lots of wavy black hair on top of his head. "Embarrassing, isn't it?"

"Want to mess with them?" asked the only girl in the squad.

"Sounds good," said the third squad member in a gruff voice. He was hunched over, with a furry cape on his back. But the strangest thing about him was the white bandages wrapped around his face. Only one eye was showing. "He knows us. Let's give him some data for that deck of cards he has. He thinks the Village in Sound is…unsound. We'll show him."

They silently began to move through the crowded room. Nobody noticed them.

The members of Squad Eight, Kiba's team,

and Squad Ten, Shikamaru's team, were mad at Naruto. They had both trained with Squad Seven at Ninja Academy.

"'None of you are gonna beat me.' The nerve of that kid!" said Squad Eight's Kiba. The ninja's dog was perched in his hair. "Little show-off."

Shikamaru of Squad Ten looked angry. "That idiot turned a room full of strangers into a room full of enemies with just one sentence," he muttered.

Sakura knew things were going to get bad. She put Naruto in a headlock.

"Stop saying stupid stuff!" she warned.

"I'm telling the truth!" Naruto protested.

Some of the ninja in the room stepped toward Naruto. They looked ready to take him up on his challenge.

"Pay no attention to my friend," Sakura said nervously. "He's got a little problem with his brain. He doesn't think right sometimes."

While everyone watched Naruto, the ninja from the Village Hidden in Sound inched closer to Kabuto.

"Shall we?" their leader asked.

WHOOSH!

WHOOSH!

WHOOSH!

The three ninja from the Sound Village raced between the ninja in the room. They moved so fast they could barely be seen.

Kabuto thought he heard a sound behind him. He turned but didn't see anything. Sakura was still scolding Naruto. Annoyed, Naruto stuck his tongue out at her.

Then...

FWWWWWAP!

The tall ninja from the Sound Village jumped into the air, almost touching the ceiling. He aimed two throwing knives called *kunai* at Kabuto.

SHIING! SHIING! They whizzed through the air. Kabuto saw them just in time. He dodged out of the way, and they stuck in the floor next to his feet.

Before Kabuto could fight back, the ninja with the bandaged face appeared right in front of him. He held two fingers in front of his bandaged lips. Then he aimed a blow at Kabuto with one powerful arm.

They're from the Sound Village, Kabuto realized. He reacted quickly. He leaned back just before the blow made contact. The ninja missed him, and Kabuto grinned.

Naruto and Sakura gawked. They were stunned.

He dodged it! They both thought at once.

Sasuke watched, impressed. *So quick I*

barely saw him move.

Then something strange happened. The lenses of Kabuto's eyeglasses suddenly shattered. The glass rained onto the floor.

The other ninja watched, curious. The bandaged ninja had not made any contact with Kabuto. So why were his glasses broken?

Kabuto had the same question. He took off his broken glasses.

I see…this kind of attack is…hmm…

"What's going on?" Sasuke asked. "He dodged the blow, but something broke his glasses."

"His nose probably got grazed," guessed Shikamaru. "Serves him right for acting like a know-it-all before."

Kabuto's body began to shudder. He fell

to his knees and threw up all over the floor.

"Aw man! He's hurling!" Naruto yelled.

"Kabuto?" Sakura was worried.

Nobody was thinking about Naruto anymore.

Now everyone stared at the ninja from the Village Hidden in Sound. They stood in front of the room, facing the others. The look on their faces was easy to read.

BRING IT ON!

NARUTO AND Sakura rushed to Kabuto's side. The ninja was still on his knees. He looked pale.

"Kabuto! Hey, bro!" Naruto said.

"Are you all right?" Sakura asked.

Kabuto didn't look up. "Yeah, I'm fine," he said in a rough voice.

"You don't look fine," Naruto remarked.

The ninja from the Sound Village looked pleased with themselves.

"You're a pushover, aren't you?" asked

the bandaged one. "Pretty sad for someone who's taken this test six times already."

"Add this to your cards," the tall ninja challenged. "The three ninja from the Sound Village will all make chunin this year."

The rest of the genin were still trying to figure out the attack they had just seen.

I know Kabuto ducked that blow, Sasuke thought. *So what happened to him? Why did he throw up?*

"Lee, what did that look like to you?" Neji asked.

Rock Lee's dark eyes studied Kabuto from under his bushy eyebrows.

"Kabuto saw through the attack," Rock Lee said. "So there must have been something else to it, some trick to make him sick."

ONNNNNNG!

A loud chiming sound filled the room. A huge cloud of smoke appeared.

"Would everybody please just shut up?"

The voice came from inside the smoke. When the air cleared, a group of tough-looking older ninja stood in the room. Each one wore a headband with the symbol of the Leaf Village on it.

The leader of the group had a face that looked like it had been carved from stone. A long scar ran from the bottom of his left eye, across his lips, and down to his chin. A smaller scar marked his right cheek. A black scarf covered his head. Over his ninja jacket and pants he wore a dark leather jacket.

"Sorry to have kept you waiting," he said. "My name is Ibiki Morino. I am the proctor and chief examiner for this exam."

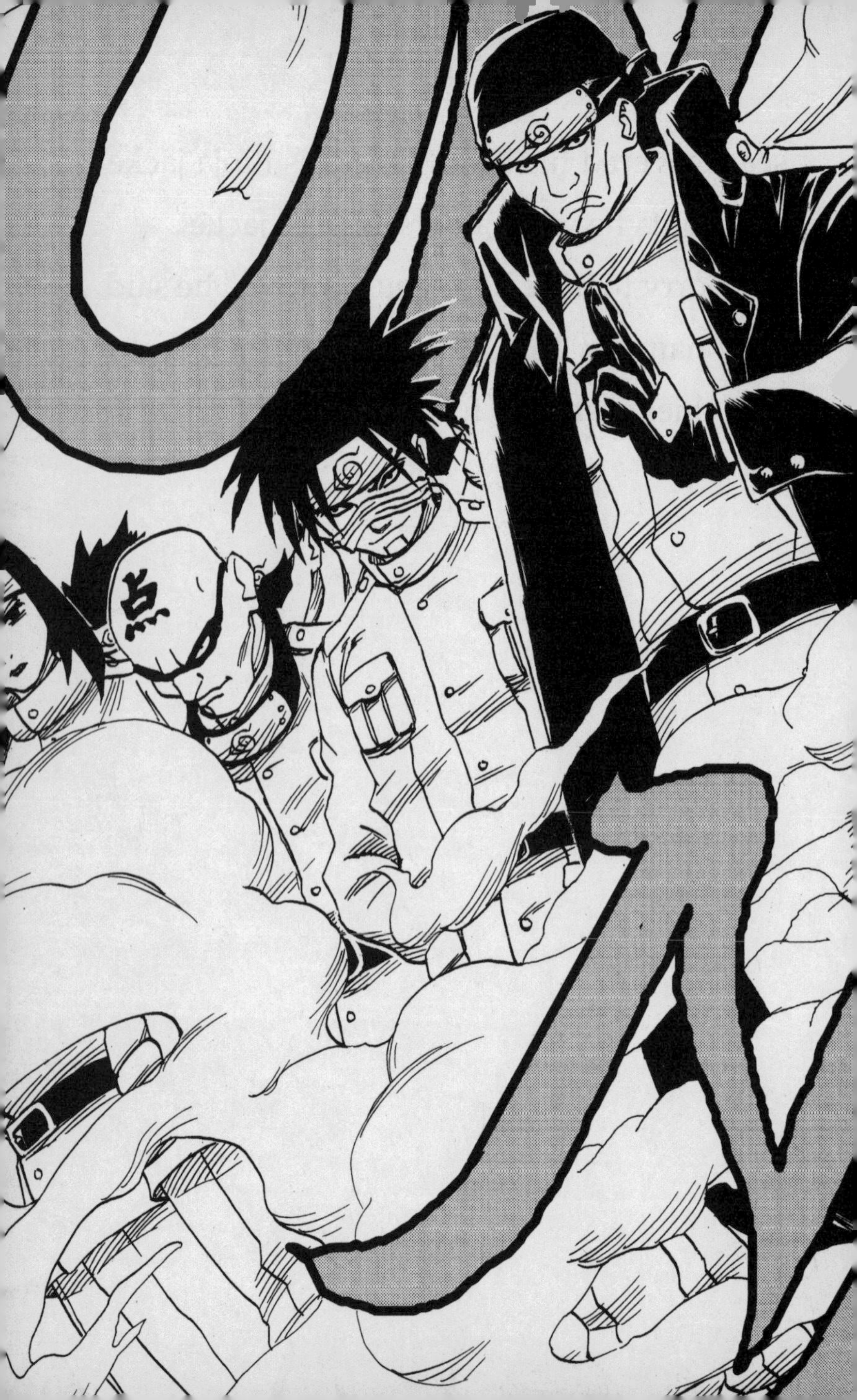
点

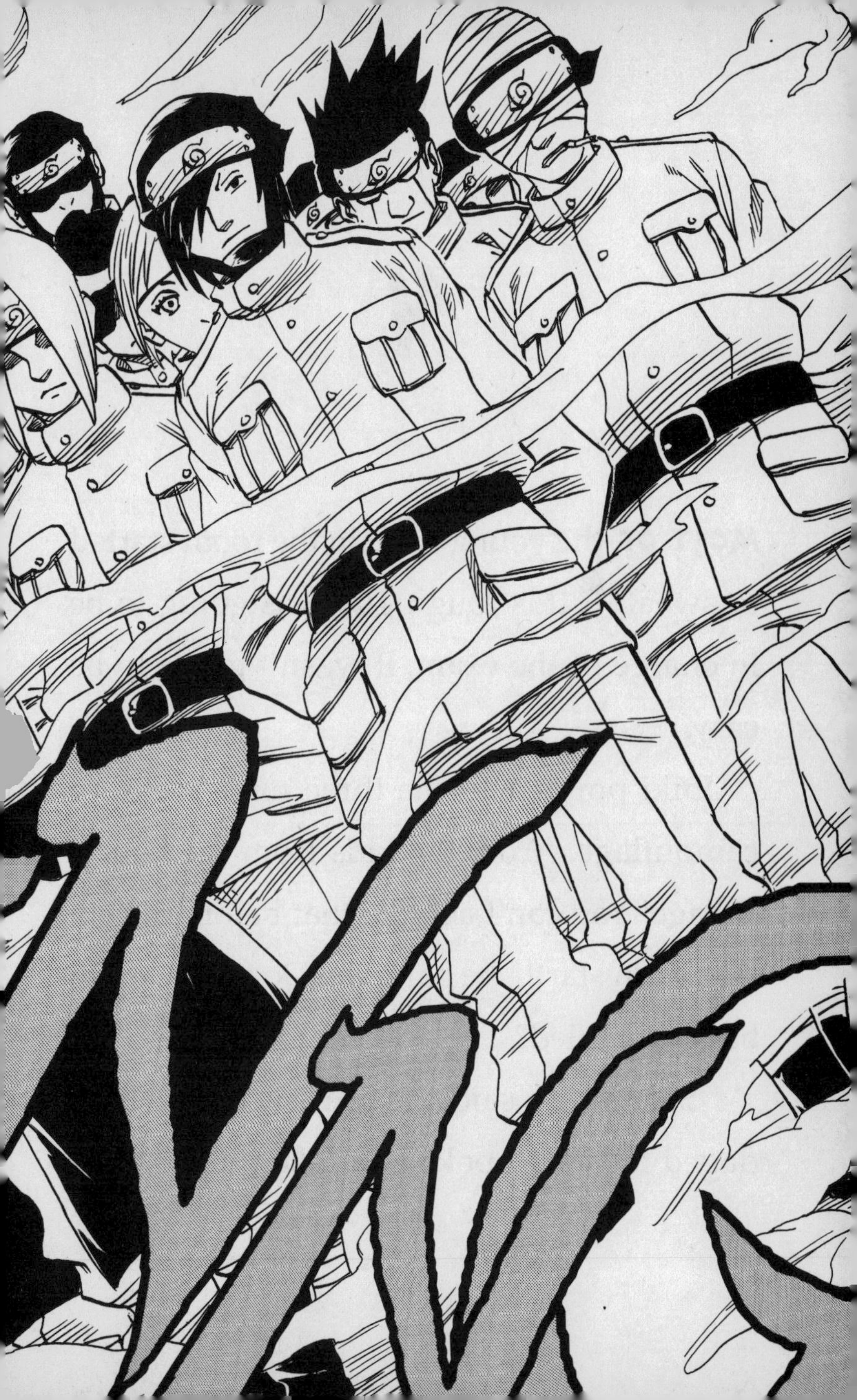

MOST OF the young ninja in the room started to sweat. If this tough guy was going to be in charge of the exam, it wasn't going to be easy.

Ibiki pointed to the three ninja wearing camouflage. "You, the kids from the Sound Village! You can't act like that before the exams even start!" he barked. "Do you want to be disqualified?"

"Sorry, sir," said the ninja with the bandaged face. He spoke in a fake polite voice.

"It's our first exam, and we got a little carried away."

"Is that so?" Ibiki asked. "Then it's time we laid down a few ground rules. From this point on, there will be no more fighting without my permission. Even then, anything that endangers the life of another is strictly forbidden."

Ibiki looked serious. "Any of you little piglets who break that rule are out. Disqualified. No second chances. Got that?"

The tall ninja from the Sound Village smirked. "So this test is for wimps?"

The rest of the proctors chuckled and sneered. The kid from the Sound Village had no idea what was going to happen.

Ibiki ignored him. "The first part of the

exam is about to begin," he announced. "Turn in your written applications. Then take a seating assignment card and report to your seat."

He held up a card with a number on it. "When everyone's seated, we'll pass out the written part of the test."

Naruto was stunned.

"A PAPER TEST?" he screamed.

Naruto thought the chunin exam would be about fighting. But a written test? He had

failed just about every written test he took at Ninja Academy.

There was nothing he could do. Naruto took his number, 53, and found his seat at one of the long tables that filled up the room. The ninja taking the exam sat side by side.

Sakura sat a few rows behind Naruto.

This must be Naruto's worse nightmare, Sakura thought. *He looks crushed!*

Naruto had his head down on the desk and his hands on top of his head.

Aw, man, we're spread out all over the room, he thought. *Now what do I do?*

"Naruto?"

Naruto looked left and saw Hinata, the third member of Squad Eight. Her blue-black hair was cut in a short style. She wore her

Leaf Village headband around her neck. Her eyes were really unusual. They were milky white, and it almost looked like she had no pupils.

"Oh, I didn't even see you, Hinata," Naruto said. Hinata was small and always quiet. She was easy to miss.

Hinata blushed and smiled. "L-let's do our best," she said.

"Papers down until I give the signal," Ibiki said. "Now listen up. There are a few rules you should know. I'll write them on the blackboard. But I'm not taking any questions, so listen up."

"Rules?" Sakura said out loud. She started to get nervous. *And no questions? Why not?*

"Rule number one," Ibiki began. "Each

one of you starts out with ten points. The test has ten questions. Each question is worth one point. For each question you get wrong, we subtract one point. So if you get three questions wrong, your total score will be seven."

And if I get all ten questions wrong, my score will be a big fat zero! Naruto thought.

"Rule number two," Ibiki went on. "This test is still a team event. The points of each member of a squad will be added together. That will determine if a team passes or fails."

Naruto slammed his head down on his desk. Sasuke and Sakura were going to hate him! If he

AND NO QUESTIONS?! WHY NOT?

RULES?

failed the test, his whole team could fail.

"Rule number three," Ibiki said. "No cheating. The proctors will be watching you. If they see anything that makes them think you're cheating, we will take away two points from *each* member of the cheater's team."

"Oh!" Sakura said. These rules were pretty tough!

"It's likely that some of you will use up all of your points before the test is over," Ibiki continued. "If that happens, you'll be asked to leave."

I get it, Sakura realized. *There's more than one way to lose a point in this test.*

One of the proctors grinned at the genin. "I'll be looking over your shoulders when you least expect it," he warned.

"If you let the proctors catch you cheating, you'll bring yourself and your friends down," Ibiki warned. "If you want to become chunin, if you want to be the best ninja you can be...then you better start acting like you already are!"

SAKURA STARTED to sweat.

Get ahold of yourself, Sakura! she thought. *Sasuke and I should be able to keep enough points for all three of us, even if Naruto gets every single answer wrong!*

"One more thing," Ibiki said. "If any person loses all ten of his or her points, that person's entire squad, no matter how the other members do, will be disqualified!"

WHAT! Sakura felt like screaming.

Even Sasuke was starting to worry.

It wouldn't matter if he aced the test. If Naruto messed up, they would all lose their chance of becoming chunin.

Naruto cringed, and sweat dripped down his face.

I can feel them from here... Both wanting to kill me already!

Sakura gripped her pencil tightly. This whole test was so unfair!

"You have one hour," Ibiki said. "Starting now!"

The sound of pencils scratching on paper filled the room.

Sakura tried to see how Naruto was doing, but all she could see was the back of Naruto's head. Things didn't look good. Naruto still held his head in his hands, frustrated.

Please, Naruto! Try to hang on to at least one of your points! Sakura begged silently.

Naruto started to laugh quietly. He just couldn't help himself.

Heh, heh, heh, he thought. *This is funny. Here I am again, facing the worst kind of enemy! Teachers didn't call me the all-time dunce for nothing!*

I earned that name on the field of battle.

To Naruto, a classroom was a battlefield.

The trick is not to show fear, Naruto coached himself. *Remain calm. Don't try to do everything at once. Look each question square in the eye. Try to find the easiest question. Separate it from the herd, and then take it down.*

He looked down at the questions, hoping to find at least one he could understand.

Sasuke was a few rows behind him. He watched Naruto, just like Sakura had.

This is so not good, he thought. *Naruto is an idiot. I just hope he doesn't panic.*

Sasuke glanced down at the test.

Whoa, first up is cryptography. Cryptography was the study of using codes to keep information secret. The question contained a complicated code. They were supposed to figure out the message. *They want us to work our butts off!*

Sasuke was starting to get a bad feeling. The way the test was set up, it was impossible for *any* squad to pass!

YOU HAVE ONE HOUR...

6

NARUTO READ the questions one by one, hoping to find an easy one. So far, he'd had no luck.

Next! he thought cheerfully. He wasn't going to give up yet.

Sakura found herself staring at Naruto. *I wonder how Naruto's doing?* she wondered. *But I've got to concentrate on my own test.*

She read the second question. It described a complicated scene. You had to figure out how far a ninja could throw a throwing star from the top of a 23.3-foot-tall tree.

Sakura frowned. The question was based on uncertain data. How strong was the ninja? Which way was the wind blowing? It was going to be really hard to answer—but not impossible.

There's no way Naruto could solve something like this, Sakura knew. *Neither could most people here. It's a killer. Of course, I can answer it.*

Naruto looked at the next question. And the next. He read every question.

His confidence left him. He turned pale.

There was no way he could answer any one of these questions. Squad Seven was sunk!

Sasuke was having the same problem. But instead of panicking, the wheels of his mind were spinning.

Well, well, he thought. *I don't know how to answer a single one of these questions. And what's the deal with number ten?*

> Question Number 10:
>
> This question will not be provided until
>
> forty-five minutes into the exam. At
>
> that time, please answer the proctor's
>
> question to the best of your ability.

Sweat poured down Naruto's face.

Man, I am in trouble! Big, big, trouble!

He felt like rolling into a ball and disappearing into the floor.

What do I do? What do I do? What do I do? What do I do? What do I do?

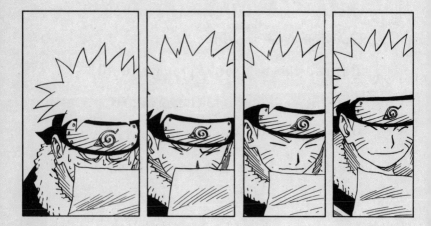

Naruto banged his head on the desk again. Next to him, Hinata gave him a sympathetic look.

There was only one thing he could do, and he knew it. He had to cheat. But how?

"I've got to be sly, sneaky," Naruto whispered.

Behind him, Sasuke glanced at the proctors. They sat in chairs all around the classroom.

They're watching us like cats watch mice, Sasuke thought. *Like they* expect *us to cheat. Those rats!*

REMAIN CALM, Naruto told himself. *Above all, be careful. My only hope is to cheat so well they don't catch me!*

Naruto regretted the thought right away. He was no cheater! He banged his head on the desk again.

No way! No way! Don't even think about it! he warned himself. *Danger! Danger! Don't even go there!*

Sasuke studied the proctors. *They're probably watching every little thing we do. Look at them making notes about us in their books. I bet they caught someone cheating already.*

He tried to remember what Ibiki had said about cheating.

If you let the proctors catch you cheating, you'll bring yourself and your friends down. If you want to become chunin, if you want to be the best ninja you can be, then you better start acting like you already are!

Sasuke froze.

Hold it! he thought. Ibiki's words held an important clue.

Unbelievable, Sasuke realized. *This is an intelligence test, all right. But it's about more than answering questions on paper.*

He looked at Naruto, wishing he could somehow send his thoughts into his squad member's brain.

Wake up, Naruto! You're history if you don't figure it out too. They're also testing our spying skills. They want us to cheat…like ninja, without getting caught!

Sasuke held his pencil in front of his face. He was excited now that he had figured it out.

Ninja must learn to uncover hidden meanings within hidden meanings. The proctors want us to cheat…and do a good job at it! The way the best ninja would if they were on a mission in the real world.

He glanced up at Ibiki. *Look at how they set up the scoring system. You get two points taken away every time you're caught cheating. But that means you get four tries before you fail. What we're being tested on is not whether we know the answers, but how skillfully we can discover them!*

Sasuke was relieved now that he knew what the test was really about. He wasn't worried about Sakura. She was smart enough to answer the questions without cheating.

Then there was Naruto. There was no way he could pass the test. Cheating was his only hope.

Come on, Naruto, Sasuke urged silently. **FIGURE IT OUT!**

SASUKE LOOKED around the room.

Any minute now, everyone who's figured out we're supposed to cheat is going to go for it, he knew. He wondered who would start first.

Red-haired Gaara from the Village Hidden in the Sand was the next to figure it out. He stared at his squad member, Kankuro.

Stop glaring at me, Kankuro thought. *I get it already!*

Gaara moved his left hand slightly. Tiny grains of sand began to swirl on his test paper. Kankuro knew Gaara was about to use one of his special ninja moves to cheat.

Gaara's started too, huh? Kankuro thought. He wasn't worried. He had plans of his own. *Don't fail me now, Scarecrow.*

But Kankuro couldn't make his move yet. The proctor sitting nearest to him gave him a warning look. Kankuro would have to wait until the time was right.

To anyone watching the group, it was pretty easy to see which ninja were able to answer the questions. They were the ones writing things down instead of staring into space, panicked. The trick would be to figure out how to copy their answers without getting caught.

Kiba from Squad Eight used his little dog, Akamaru, to help him. From his perch on Kiba's head, Akamaru could clearly see the other test papers. He saw the answers, then gave them to Kiba in code.

WOOF! WOOF! WOOF! Akamaru barked.

"Good boy, Akamaru!" Kiba whispered. "Next is question number four..."

Squad Eight's Shino was also using a partner to help him cheat. Shino wore dark black glasses and pulled the collar of his jacket up over the bottom of his face. He sent his partner, a bee, to look at the paper of a ninja wearing glasses. The bee flew back to Shino and landed on his finger. Then the bee began to buzz.

"Excellent!" Shino hissed. "Tell me more."

Like Sakura, Tenten from Rock Lee's squad knew many of the answers. But she knew her teammates would need help. Luckily, Tenten was sitting under the light fixture on the ceiling. A series of glass panels circled the light bulbs. Tenten moved her test paper until it was reflected perfectly in one of the panels. Now she just had to get Rock Lee to see it.

Tenten made some hand signals that only she and her squad members knew.

Lee, if you can see it, adjust your headband.

Rock Lee casually reached back and tightened his headband. Tenten grinned. It was going to work!

The bandaged ninja from the Village Hidden in Sound had another approach. He zeroed in on the ninja wearing glasses, listening to the sound his pencil made on the paper.

From the rhythm and the number of strokes, I can make out the words, he thought. *Got it!*

Neji from Rock Lee's squad had the same milky white eyes as Hinata. The ninja in front of him was writing answers on his paper. Neji knew just what to do. He would use his *kekkei genkai*—a special ninja skill passed down through a ninja family.

Byakugan! The All-Seeing Eye!

Neji's eyes began to glow. He focused on the back of the ninja in front of him. As his power kicked in, he could see right through the ninja. The answers were his!

Neji was not the only ninja in the room with a kekkei genkai. Sasuke had one too. He scanned the room, looking for someone he could cheat from. Then he spotted the ninja with the glasses.

That's the one. I'm going to copy his every move!

Sasuke focused all of his energy into his kekkei genkai—the Sharingan Copy Eye*!*

Sasuke's eyes turned red. Black, tear-dropped shaped symbols swirled around his pupils. With the Sharingan Eye, Sasuke could copy the moves of another ninja. He normally used the attack in battle—but now he was using it to copy the ninja as he wrote down the answers.

The hour for the test was quickly passing. Naruto still hadn't figured out that he was supposed to cheat. The loud *tick-tock* of the clock burned into his brain.

I'm almost out of time, he thought desperately. *Aaargh!*

He yanked on his hair in frustration. He didn't want to cheat. But what else was he going to do?

Rats! he thought. *If I don't cheat, I'm dead anyway!* It was an impossible situation.

Then something whizzed past his ear.

Naruto froze. Was that a kunai?

THOCK! The throwing knife jammed into the desk of the ninja behind him. The ninja screamed in fright and jumped back.

That was close! Naruto thought.

The stunned ninja stared at the knife sticking into his test paper.

"Wh-what was that for?" he stammered angrily.

"**THAT'S FIVE STRIKES**," one of the proctors said calmly, "and you're out."

The ninja turned pale. "No way!"

"Take your teammates with you," the

proctor said calmly. "Leave this classroom.
NOW!"

9

"YOU'RE DONE here. Move it!" the proctor barked at the three ninja as they sulked out.

Yipe! That was too close. No way I'm going to risk cheating. Not alone, Naruto thought.

"N-Naruto!"

It was Hinata, whispering beside him.

"You can look at my paper if you want to," she said softly. Her cheeks were pink.

"Hunh?" Naruto was shocked.

Hinata was a member of Squad Eight. Along with Squad Ten and Squad Seven, they

YOU CAN LOOK AT MY PAPER, IF YOU WANT TO...

were the youngest ninja taking the test. Each squad wanted to prove they were the best.

"Naruto, please look at my answers," Hinata whispered.

What's Hinata talking about? Why would she want to help me? Naruto wondered.

He quickly glanced over at her. Hinata had pushed her paper toward him. He could see everything.

No way! Naruto quickly looked away. It must be some kind of trick.

He put his head down on his desk and thought about this. *That would be such a dirty trick, but Hinata's not like that. Unless Kiba and Shino made her do it.*

"Level with me," Naruto hissed. "What's in it for you if you help me?"

Hinata blushed even more. "It's...it's just..."

Hinata nervously touched the tips of her index fingers together. She couldn't look at Naruto.

"I...you..." She gulped. "I don't want you to leave so soon, Naruto."

Naruto gave her a blank look. He didn't get it.

Embarrassed, Hinata started to talk quickly. "Well, you know there are only nine of us newbies, and we don't know what we're facing. Odds will be better for all of us if we stick together. At least for now."

Naruto grinned. "Oh, okay. I guess that makes sense. Sorry for doubting you."

He looked down at his paper. *Boy, this is my lucky day! Good thing Hinata was next to me!*

Naruto slyly peeked at her paper. All he had to do was write down the answers...

Scratch...scratch...scratch...

Naruto turned. The proctor sitting nearest to him was writing something in his notebook. Was he taking notes on Naruto? Naruto started to sweat all over again.

It was just too risky. Naruto decided to play it cool.

"Hinata, don't you get it?" he whispered.

"Hunh?" Now it was Hinata's turn to be surprised.

Naruto grinned. "A world-class ninja like me just isn't the kind of guy who cheats!" he said.

Hinata looked worried. She knew that if Naruto didn't cheat, he would fail.

"Besides, if I get busted, I don't want you to pay for helping me," he went on.

Hinata couldn't believe it. Naruto didn't

want to get her in trouble. That was so sweet!

Anyway, if I get caught doing the crime, Sakura and that jerk Sasuke are gonna have to do the time, Naruto thought to himself. *I can't afford to mess up here.*

"I'm sorry I bothered you," Hinata said.

She looked down at her paper.

"Hey, no problem," Naruto replied.

He sounded cool, but inside he was falling apart.

Great, she believed me. Now I've got my honor...but I'm toast!

Tick-tock. Tick-tock. Tick-tock...

Naruto glared at the clock, wishing he could make it stop. *The test's been going on for half an hour. Only another half left.*

Naruto's teammates were doing their best

to pass. Sakura used her brains to answer the questions. Sasuke used his Sharingan Eye to copy the answers without being caught.

But there was nothing Naruto could do. Well, almost nothing.

There were only nine questions on the paper. Ibiki had said the last question would be asked at the end of the test. If he got that one question right, he still had a chance.

At this point, the last question is my only hope!

10

SAKURA FINISHED writing the answer to question nine.

That's it! I've answered them all! Sakura felt confident. *There's nothing left for me to do but wait for the tenth question.*

Sasuke was pleased with himself as well. His hand quickly moved on its own, writing down the answers on his test paper.

I've been writing nonstop, he thought. *I was going to try to mimic two or three other students to be on the safe side. But I hit the target dead center on my first try.*

In one of the back rows, blonde-haired Ino kept an eye on Sakura. The two girls had been rivals when they went to Ninja Academy.

It looks like Sakura has finally stopped writing, Ino realized. *Time for me to make my move.*

She held two fingers in front of her lips.

Sakura, your wide forehead and big brain have earned my respect, Ino thought. *So you ought to feel honored that you're going to be the target of my signature technique. Here it comes…*

Ino slumped down on her desk. Her squad members, lazy Shikamaru and chubby Choji, watched her.

Ino's asleep. She must be using that technique of hers, Shikamaru realized.

No one can resist her when she starts that

astral-projection stuff, thought Choji.

Sakura gasped. She could feel it. Something…or someone…had entered her mind!

Ino had projected herself inside Sakura. She laughed.

Thanks for letting me possess you like this and see all of your answers, Sakura, Ino thought. She picked up the paper and started to read. *Have to memorize this quickly, before I get caught. Next I'll possess Shikamaru and Choji and write the answers for them. Clever little me!*

…SO YOU OUGHT TO FEEL HONORED… ♡

SAKURA… YOUR BROAD BROW AND BIG BRAIN HAVE EARNED MY RESPECT…

Ino didn't get caught. But she was one of the lucky ones. The proctors were throwing out team after team for cheating. Soon, thirteen squads had been eliminated.

Some of the ninja got angry.

"Cheated five times? What kind of proof do you have?" one shouted. "How could you possibly watch this many students at once?"

The proctor who had nabbed him was a slim ninja who wore his headband over his eyes like a blindfold. He picked up the ninja in one hand, slamming him against the wall.

"Listen up and listen good!" the proctor shouted to the class. "We proctors have been chosen for this because we're the best. We miss nothing. Got that, kids?"

Nobody answered. They nervously turned

back to their test papers.

Gaara from the Sand Village looked calm—too calm. Ibiki eyed him suspiciously. Gaara held the two fingers of his right hand under his chin. A hand sign like that usually signaled the start of a ninja move.

Hmmmf. That brat is up to something, Ibiki thought. *Whatever he's doing, he's barely moving. For a rookie, he's amazing.*

Gaara touched the fingers of his right hand to his left eye. He held his left hand, palm up, on his knee. Grains of sand swirled in his open palm. The sand slowly formed into an eyeball.

POK! Gaara's eyeball appeared in his left hand!

My third eye is now open, Gaara thought

calmly.

He squeezed his left hand tightly. Grains of sand spilled out. Gaara blew on the sand, and it floated across the room to one of the ninja. The sand landed in the ninja's left eye.

"Ow!" the ninja exclaimed. "Something's in my eye!"

He rubbed his eyes. The sand formed into Gaara's eyeball again. It floated down and hovered over the ninja's paper. Even though he was sitting rows away, Gaara could see the paper with his eyeball. He quickly wrote down the test answers.

Gaara's squad member Kankuro was ready

to put his plan in place. He raised his hand.

"May I go to the bathroom?" he asked.

A proctor stepped forward. "Of course. I will go with you."

"Why not?" Kankuro asked cheerfully.

The proctor put Kankuro in handcuffs. As soon as they went into the bathroom, the proctor's face began to crumble, as if it were made of stone. The proctor wasn't real! It was some jutsu Kankuro had used to cheat!

"Nice work, Scarecrow," Kankuro said with a grin. "Now give me all of the answers, starting with number one."

Back in the classroom, Ibiki looked at the clock.

Now that we've weeded out the worst slackers, let's move on to the most important question, the chief examiner thought. *Forty-five minutes has passed. It's time.*

Ibiki walked to the center of the room.

"Get ready for the tenth question!" he announced.

Naruto's eyes were open as wide as they could go. Sweat poured down his face.

It was all up to this, the tenth question. If he couldn't answer it, he would fail. Even worse, Squad Seven would fail too. They would have to remain junior ninja for another year.

Naruto clenched his fists. He was as ready as he was going to get.

Let's go!

Ninja Terms

Nindo
A shinobi's *ninja way*, a moral code a ninja follows to stay on the path of good.

Jutsu
Jutsu means "arts" or "techniques." Sometimes referred to as *ninjutsu*, which means more specifically the jutsu of a ninja.

Bunshin
Translated as "doppelganger," this is the art of creating multiple versions of yourself.

Sensei
Teacher

Taijutsu
A physical type of jutsu.

Chunin Selection Exam
The test that determines which young ninja become journeymen.

Cryptography
The study of using codes to hide secret information.

About the Authors

Author/artist **Masashi Kishimoto** was born in 1974 in rural Okayama Prefecture, Japan. After spending time in art college, he won the Hop Step Award for new manga artists with his manga *Karakuri* (Mechanism). Kishimoto decided to base his next story on traditional Japanese culture. His first version of *Naruto*, drawn in 1997, was a one-shot story about fox spirits; his final version, which debuted in *Weekly Shonen Jump* in 1999, quickly became the most popular ninja manga in Japan. This book is based on that manga.

. . . . . .

Tracey West is the author of more than 150 books for children and young adults, including the *Pixie Tricks* and *Scream Shop* series. An avid fan of cartoons, comic books, and manga, she has appeared on the New York Times Best Seller List as the author of the Pokémon chapter book adaptations. She currently lives with her family in New York State's Hudson Valley.

The Story of Naruto continues in:
Chapter Book II
The Tenth Question

Naruto, Sasuke, and Sakura are well into

the first test of the chunin exam. If they

pass, they'll become the next level of trained

ninja! But now the rules of the exam have

changed. They'll have to work harder

then ever to answer the Tenth Question!

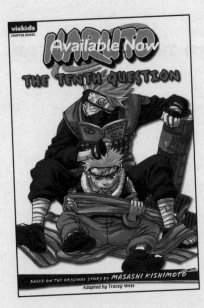

COLLECT THEM ALL!

#1 THE BOY NINJA
#2 THE TESTS OF A NINJA
#3 THE WORST JOB
#4 THE SECRET PLAN
#5 BRIDGE OF COURAGE
#6 SPEED
#7 THE NEXT LEVEL
#8 INTRUDERS
#9 THE CHALLENGERS
#10 THE FIRST TEST

COMING SOON!

#11 THE TENTH QUESTION

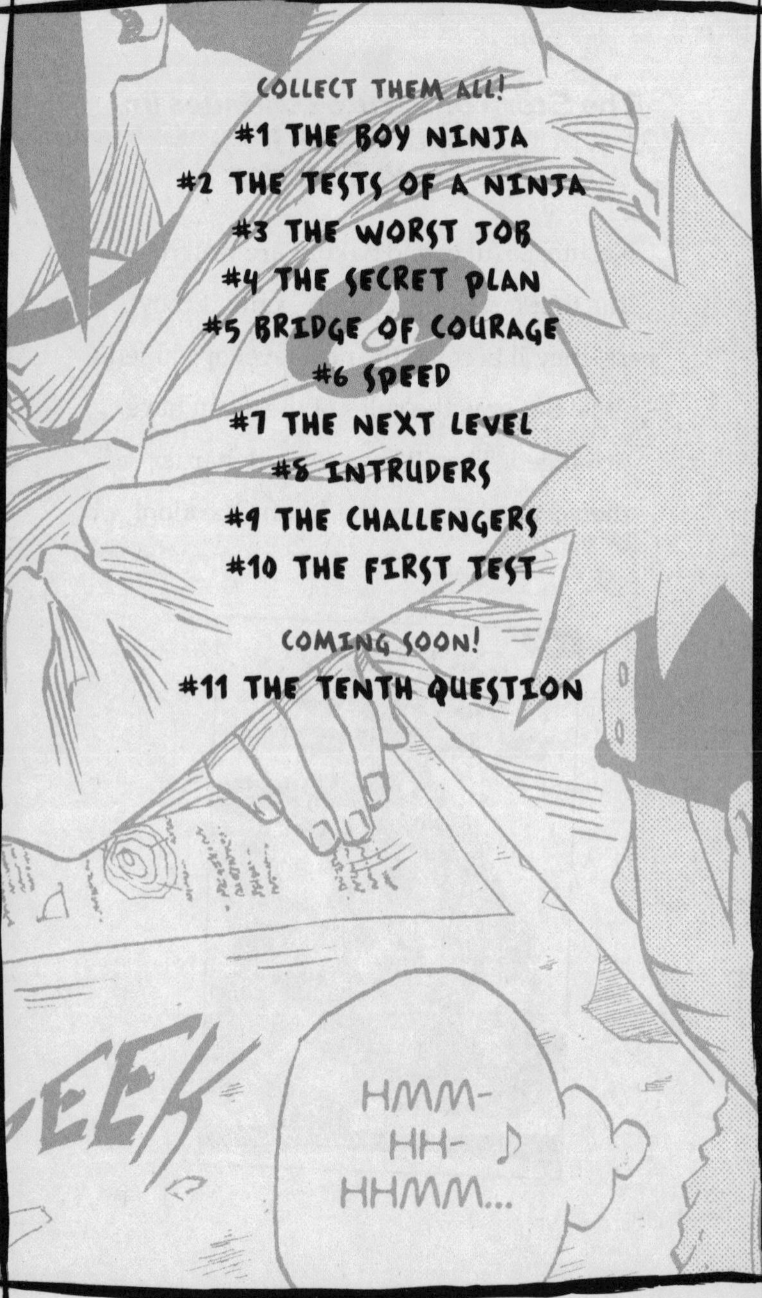
EEK
HMM-
HH- ♪
HHMM...